AF507805

3

Dedicated to dreaming

This book is a work of fiction. Names, characters, incidences, and places are either products of the author's imagination or are used fictitiously. Any resemblance to actual events, locales, or persons, living or dead, is entirely coincidental.

No parts of this publication may be reproduced, distributed, or transmitted in any form or by any means, including photocopying, recording, or other electronic or mechanical methods, without the prior written permission of the publisher, except as permitted by the US copyright law. For permission requests, contact GK Wilson at gkwilson.author@gmail.com

Edited by Forward Reviews

Cover design by Chad Lutzke

Copyright 2024 by GK Wilson

First Edition September 2024 in the United States of America

ISBN (Paperback) 9798339083856, 9798330427741

ISBN (Hardback) 9798339089780, 9798330423743

Silence

By

GK Wilson

Swamp:

A tract of wet spongy land unfit for cultivation having a growth of certain types of trees…and other things.

Chapter 1

Before it heard the first footsteps of humans, it lived and played as it always had, running in the wind and through the branches of trees heavy with Spanish moss. It delighted in the dark recesses of the swamp when the sun was up and, at night, stretched itself out to rest across the water of its pond. It observed the world with curiosity and watched as its home became crowded with animals that, acting by some unwritten laws of nature, would sometimes attack and eat each other. It never wondered at these things and wasn't upset by them, as they seemed to be no more than the natural rhythm of existence. It had no concept of time. Nor did it have a name.

But all that changed when what it came to know as humans entered its home. With their gangliness and crude ways, this new thing seemed to it like it wouldn't survive for long in the shadowy regions of the swamp. It seemed, with its outer body having no protection against the rough elements, too soft and, with its yielding feet, to be too slow compared to the reptiles and other creeping things that also called the swamp home. Yet, slowly, it became enamored with them as their numbers flourished instead of dwindled. As the sun rose and fell, it began to understand the concept of their days and years, learned their language, and entertained itself by producing the same sounds that they did in the only way that it could, with the energy of its thoughts. It, above all, took pleasure in creating the softest tones it heard, those of the small children.

Eventually, it began to attempt to appear like them. In the same way that it would stretch itself out across the water of its pond, it practiced gathering itself together into a form that resembled the humans. Then, when it was ready, it started to show itself to them. At first, only to the ones that had lived the longest. But they had been afraid of it, seeing its movements as unnatural and its inability to speak using the mouth that it had created as frightening. To its sadness, only a few had been able to hear it speaking to them with its mind at all, and those few, instead of welcoming it, had warned the others against it. It began to play with the younger ones instead. Many more of them could hear it, and so it started to make itself look more and more like them, learning to blend in with the groups of children so well that it could join in their games without being noticed by the older ones.

As its fondness grew, it began to want these tiny people to stay with it forever, not age and leave like all living things eventually did. So, in its misguided love, it decided to keep the little ones young eternally by guiding its very favorites among them to its pond and then enticing them to the center of its resting place, where it would spread itself out across the top of the water and never let them leave.

This caused a great outcry from the older humans. It listened to them from afar as they called it things like evil, and this made it angry. So, in retaliation, it started to show itself to them in forms that it knew would terrify them, amused by their fear and confusion. It was then that the one they called their healer began to do things that forced it to stay away, taking from its very swamp elements of the earth and blending them together, then burning them into the air where the scents would confuse it, making it impossible for it to keep its human form and causing it to lose its sense of where it was. The healer also gave it a name. Calling it after its inability to use its mouth to talk, the healer named it Silence.

Over time its anger turned into hate for the humans and what it saw as their greed in wanting to keep all of their small ones for themselves. It consoled itself with its thought about what it knew of nature. That the healer, like all living things, would eventually pass from the earth. So, it rested on its pond and waited, but as the healer grew near death, the leaders, knowing that a threat still existed, moved the entire camp far away from the swamp, where it could no longer see or hear them.

Time passed for it again, only now it had a concept of days and years like humans did. Occasionally, new humans would make homes near its swamp and walk close by, and it would hear the voices of the old ones telling a story about it, a story meant to frighten the little ones into staying away. But still, every once in a while, it would catch the tinkling of tiny voices nearby and, with great excitement, gather itself together and call out to them.

14

Chapter 2

Matilde sat on a wooden kitchen chair on her small front porch, listening to the birds singing to each other from the branches of the magnolia tree. She shifted slightly in her seat, rebalancing the stone bowl and wooden spoon she held on her lap. Inside the bowl was a mixture of herbs, dirt from her mother's resting place under the magnolia tree, and coarse salt. With a sigh, she picked up the spoon and began grinding together the contents. As she worked, she let her mind drift back forty years to when she was a thirteen-year-old girl: her mother had moved them to the small town of Deep Creek, located in what the townspeople called the far-southern end of the state and close to a swamp. With stifling humidity in the summer and unpredictable snowstorms in the winter, it was a place she hadn't liked. She had wanted to return to Louisiana, where they had moved from, but her mother would hear none of it.

They had moved many times during Matilde's younger years. Her mother struggled to fit in at each new location. They would be welcome at first; her mother always seemed to draw people to her who needed help, and she would aid them with her home remedies. But eventually, they would notice that she could help them with other things as well, things that fell outside the realm of minor physical ailments and were not talked about in polite company. While these people were always willing to accept what help she gave with their colds and arthritic hands, they weren't willing to accept the boundaries that her mother would lay down when performing remedies for them of a darker nature. If any type of fixing was asked for that took away the free actions or thoughts of another, then her mother would refuse to help them. It was then that they would turn on her. It would always start the same: a rumor here and there, then slowly, these little rumors would coagulate into an ugly description of her mother that they would spread through the town. Once this description was firmly set in place, it would only be a matter of time before they, the ones who had been told no, would start to ostracize her mother from the community, and this treatment of her mother always trickled down to Matilde. The children of people that her mother once knew would no longer play with Matilde in the schoolyard. Weekends once spent getting ice cream at the parlor in town would turn into quiet days at home. It was then that her mother would start looking for another place for them to go, knowing that just past this quiet existed the threat of violence.

So, in her thirteenth year, they had come to Deep Creek, and her mother had secured them a small house just past the edge of town, close to a swamp. They had lived quietly at first, and although unhappy with the area, Matilde had found solace in the fact that the townspeople were polite and mostly kept to themselves. The requests for her mother's help still came eventually, but the people of Deep Creek accepted Matilde's mother's boundaries and her unwillingness to meddle in the darker forms of her craft. Maybe because, for the first time Matilde could remember, other people in the small community had the same gifts her mother had, giving the townspeople other places to turn when her mother told them no.

It was the summer of her fourteenth year when trouble came, but not in the usual way. It had been late June, and Matilde was working in their garden, moving slowly between the rows of plants, pulling a stray weed here and there when she'd heard murmuring in the early morning breeze. It had seemed to be calling to her with a voice as sweet as honey from the hive, speaking words she hadn't quite been able to make out. She'd turned her head to hear the melodic tones more clearly, then froze as her mind had found a feeling within the melody that shouldn't have been there. Hate and evil had glided just under the vibration of the sweet call. Goosebumps had risen on her arms, and a current not unlike electricity had raced along the surface of her skin. She'd whimpered as the murmuring continued, tears coming to her eyes as a feeling of darkness had gripped her. She'd turned towards her house and seen her mother standing at the back door, a look of concern clouding her features as she had looked intently past Matilde toward the swamp's edge.

"Come in here, child," she'd said.

Matilde's feet, which had felt rooted to the spot, broke free at her mother's command, and she ran to her. She had hidden behind her, then peered cautiously over her shoulder toward the swamp and asked in a shaky voice, "What is it?"

Her mother had stared toward the swamp. Her eyes had opened wide, searching past the depth of air and light, into the spaces in between. Then, suddenly, she'd taken a sharp breath, and her body went rigid.

"Mama?" Matilde had asked, alarmed.

A look of fear had taken over her mother's features, and she seemed to Matilde to be unable to move. Matilde had taken hold of her and dragged her to the couch, where she laid her down and covered her with a light blanket. She had tried to get her to drink some cool water but couldn't. Then she had tried to get her mother to talk to her, but she wouldn't. Scared and not knowing what to do, Matilde had decided to walk into town and find help. She had just opened their front door and was about to leave the house when she heard her mother behind her.

"Don't go out there," she'd said.

Matilde had turned and gone to kneel by her side. She'd taken her mother's hand in her own, asking, "What's wrong?"

Her mother's gaze had been unfocused as she gripped Matilde's hand and insisted, "Don't leave this house. I've laid down protection all around this house but not in the yard. Don't leave this house."

"I won't," Matilde had repeatedly reassured her as night fell. Eventually, Matilde had fallen asleep, sitting on the floor, her head resting on the couch.

When she had awoken the following morning, her mother had no longer been in the room with her. Matilde had found her in the kitchen. She'd had the same stone bowl Matilde now held in her lap sitting on the table and a variety of herbs and salts spread out along the countertops. She'd turned to Matilde and said, "We need to go to the graveyard."

That day, her mother had taught her how to blend elements and minerals from the earth to create a circle of protection meant to confuse and redirect anything that tried to cross it with ill will, and she had told her about things of eternal nature and dark energies. She had talked all day as they'd worked. Then, that evening, when they'd finally sat down to rest, she'd told Matilde something that had been hard for her to hear: that sometimes, within families, in the same way that eye color is passed down from a parent to a child, a gift is sometimes passed down through the blood.

Matilde had listened all day without interruption but she had objected profusely to that. As much as she loved her mother, she had not wanted to be like her. Still, her mother had insisted, telling Matilde that she could deny to herself what she had heard and felt earlier if that was what she wanted to do, but the effect would be the same as a woman who colors her hair. The outward appearance would be different, but the underlying color would remain, and in the same way that this false coloring would require regular maintenance, so too would lying to herself require an exhausting amount of mental maintenance.

Her mother hadn't known what was in the swamp. Only that it was dark, and it had called for Matilde. They had circled the area outside their yard with their mixture almost every day, and all was quiet for a while.

Later, her mother had asked the people she knew in the town whether they had heard anything odd about the swamp. People had initially been slow to talk about it, but eventually, they opened up. They had told Matilde and her mother that if you crossed the field behind their house, entered the swamp, and went in about a quarter of a mile, you would come to a clearing where a pond fed by an underground water source glistened and reflected a beautiful array of the surrounding trees and sky, but that there was a strangeness to this pond that no one could explain. Like that, no matter how windy a day, the pond's water stayed flat, and the clearing was too quiet, almost completely devoid of any of the sounds of nature surrounding it. According to local folklore, the first people to ever live in the area had called the place Silence. No one ever went there due to the pond's oddities and the stories of the area's past.

One of the stories told about troubles when the buildings and houses of the town itself were erected. When Deep Creek was first founded, the workers who had come to build the stores and houses brought their wives and children with them. They stayed in small rows of simple, slapped-together dwellings that were more shacks than houses. They had stood between where Matilde's home sat now and the swamp. There were ten children among the families who came, and they had stayed for two years erecting the town center along with the three houses near the swamp. During those two years, three of the children went missing, and two more were found at the edge of the swamp, their life gone from them. The house where Matilde and her mother lived and the two located next to it were the only three homes the workers would build close to the swamp, refusing to build more in that location despite significant pressure from the town's planners for them to do so. As the story went, the workers believed something lived in the swamp and had called their children away from them, and they'd abandoned the budding town before the building was done. The town's building planner had gone through a total of four different crews before the town was complete. Each time the crews had stayed in the rows of shacks near the swamp, and each time, there had been losses, and no crew supervisor would build more houses next to the swamp. So, the three houses stood alone. On top of this, as the years passed, no family that had moved into any of these three houses stayed for very long, and over the years, children had been lost. When Matilde and her mother had moved into one of the houses, the people in Deep Creek had assumed they wouldn't be staying long either.

Time passed, and Matilde and her mother mostly kept to themselves. The townspeople visited occasionally, requesting her mother's help, but they were not ugly towards them. After a while, as Matilde's senses sharpened and she began to experience life more and more in the way that her mother did, she started to accept her gifts and began helping her mother, learning from her how to mix more than just protective circles. She'd still heard the murmuring occasionally over the next few years, but as long as she didn't pass the edge of their backyard where their boundary lay, its sweet cadence sounded distorted to her. Matilde tried never to go into the field past their backyard or go close to the swamp's edge. Not even after she had grown into an adult and stopped hearing the murmurs altogether.

However, her mother would. Armed with a single candle and a small pouch filled with something that she called "Binding" which contained, amongst other things, a single drop of her own blood, or the payment as she called it, would walk determinedly to the edge of the swamp, light the candle, and burn the pouch. For a long time, Deep Creek didn't experience the heartache of even one missing child.

Then her mother had died. Matilde had had her cremated and spread the ashes under the magnolia tree so she would always be close to the only long-term home that either of them had ever known.

Matilde stopped grinding her mixture in the bowl to let the grief at the memory of the loss of her mother pass through her. Then she returned to her task, gaining solace from the familiar scent of the herbs. The past five years had been welcomingly quiet for her. Every few days, she ground a fresh mixture to pour around her yard, and she had taken part-time work at a shop in town to fill some of her hours. Yet, for some reason, on this morning, she was uneasy. She sighed and set her stone bowl and spoon beside her, then crossed her arms over her chest and leaned back, closing her eyes. The heat had begun to climb, and she could feel the press of humidity that always came with it. A slight breeze blew over her, but instead of bringing some relief from the heat, she felt a warning in it. She opened her eyes and instinctually looked toward the magnolia tree. She thought she heard her mother say, "Wake up, child."

She turned her head to the side, listening intently in the way that her mother had taught her. Not to the obvious sounds of the world, like birds chirping or a car in the distance, but to the sounds in between, and there it was. The sweet cadence she'd heard all those years ago carrying through the air, singing toward whoever might hear it. She shuddered as its name came to her. Silence.

Chapter 3

Saturday afternoon, Lindsey Colson pulled the final strip of packing tape across the top of the last moving box. "There," she said aloud as she patted the tape down, securing it in place. She moved the box to the pile of things she was taking with her, stacked beside her bedroom door in her mom's mobile home. The sound of morning cartoons caught her attention, and she called out, "Allie, honey, get your stuff ready. We're going to go soon." She heard the quick footsteps of her daughter coming towards her, and she turned just as her little girl careened into her and wrapped her chubby little arms around her waist.

"Whoa, what's this?" she asked laughingly, gazing down into her daughter Allison's bright eyes and trusting smile.

"It's me!" replied Allie with a giggle.

"Well, I know it's you, silly, but why are you still in your pajamas? It's after lunch. I told you to get changed hours ago."

Allison looked at her mom, frowned, and said, "No, I'm not going. I'm going to stay with grandma."

Lindsey unwrapped her daughter's arms from around her waist, leaned down, and said, "Allie, now we've been over this again and again. You can't stay here with grandma. You're coming with me."

Allie stuck out her bottom lip and glared at her mom, placing her tiny fists on her hips.

Lindsey stood back up and pointed one finger at Allie, saying in her sternest mom voice, "Now, you, young lady, are going to get dressed like you were told, and you're going to get your bag, and we're going to go."

Allie's bottom lip quivered, and quick tears filled her eyes.

Lindsey dropped her hand and pulled Allie to her. "Don't be sad, honey," she said. "It's a big change, I know, but it isn't that far, and Grandma can come visit us whenever she wants. Sometimes, we'll come here and visit her too, okay?"

Allie sniffled and nodded her head.

Lindsey let go of Allie and said, "Now go on and do as I tell you. It's going to be a big day for us. We're going to move to a new house, and you're going to have your own room, so you won't have to share one with Mom anymore. Now, won't that be nice? And you'll make lots of new friends."

Allie didn't respond and instead pushed the thin strands of her light brown hair away from her face and stomped from the room.

My little girl is so stubborn, Lindsey thought, then laughed, remembering how often she had heard her mom use those exact words. She heard the radio in the mobile home's small kitchen turn on and knew that her mom was there and that she probably wanted to talk with her. She left her bedroom and crossed the mobile home's small living area into the kitchen, where she found her mom smoking a cigarette at the table. She looked up as Lindsey came over and sat down next to her.

"So, this is it?" her mom asked with forced happiness. Her hand shook as she flicked the ash off the end of her cigarette into the ashtray on the table, "You're a big girl now going out on your own with your daughter to live in your own house," she said, attempting to smile. Her eyes met Lindsey's and held them for a moment. Then she reached forward, and they hugged each other tightly. "I am going to miss you so much," she said.

Lindsey said, "You can still change your mind. You can come with us. There are three bedrooms, Mom, and one of those can be yours."

Her mom shook her head, pulling back, then wiped the tears from her eyes and said, "No, you've got to start your own life now, and I understand." She gave a short laugh and added, "One day, I'm going to be an old lady, and that third bedroom is going to be where you're going to have to take care of me whether you want to or not!"

Lindsey leaned back in her chair and said, "Well, you're welcome to come before that, Mom. Just remember, if you change your mind…"

Her mom looked around the mobile home and said, "No, I'm home here. This is my place, but I'll think about it. Maybe in a year or two, once you're settled, things will be different. Who knows, but I'm going to miss you and Allie something awful."

At that moment, Allie stomped into the kitchen with her bag. She dropped it on the floor and said, "I'm ready."

Lindsey noticed that Allie had changed from her pajamas into her Halloween costume from the year before and a pair of cowboy boots. She and her mother looked at each other. Lindsey rolled her eyes, and her mother sighed.

"Come here, baby," her mom said.

Allie sighed, went to stand before her grandma, and folded her small arms across her chest.

"Now, Allie, don't be like that. You know that Grandma loves you, and I will come to see you as soon as you're settled in your house, and you know what else?" she asked.

Allie shook her head.

"I'm going to bring you a present, and it's gonna be something special to make you feel right at home."

"You promise?" Allie asked.

"Yes, I do, and you know what else? It's only going to take a few weeks for the two of you to get settled in. Then I'm going to come see you and stay the night." she added.

That made Allie smile, and she walked back over to her bag, picked it up, and stood by the door.

"Hold on a minute, Allie," Lindsey said. "I have to get just a few more things, and then I'll be ready to start packing the car."

"There's nothing more you need to get," her mom said, stubbing her cigarette in the ashtray. "We've delayed this long enough. It's time. Besides, you're not taking very much with you now anyway, are you?"

"I've got pretty much everything I need," Lindsey agreed. "The house already has some furniture in it, and I'll pick up dishes and things like that when we get there."

She and Lindsey rose from the table, and Lindsey walked to her room.

"What was the name of the town again?" She heard her mom call.

"Deep Creek," Lindsey answered.

"That's a funny name for a town," her mom replied. "But the summers shouldn't be as hot as they are down here. How many hours' drive is it again?"

"It's right at about five," Lindsey called back. "I thought it was a funny name, too, so I looked it up. I guess the area had been called that for a long time, and then when the town was built, they kept the name." Lindsey added, "When you come to visit, you're going to have to stay for a while, not just overnight. That's too far to drive then turn around and go home the very next day."

Her mom appeared in her doorway and said, "I was hoping you would say that. What made you decide to move to a place so far away anyway?" she asked gently. "I mean, was it something about here…or me?"

"Mom, no!" Lindsey replied quickly. "I'm just twenty-five years old now, and Allie is almost nine, and I've waitressed so many tables around this small town while I was getting my degree that everybody just knows me as their waitress, and that was fine before I finished college, but now that I have finally finished, I don't want to be around the same people whose breakfast orders I know by heart. I want to make a new start for us somewhere that nobody can look at me and say "Hey, look, there's Lindsey, do you remember her? She's the girl who dropped out of high school." And you know it as well as I do that it doesn't matter to any of these people that I've changed my life now. That's all they'll ever see: a drop-out and their waitress. But this house in Deep Creek is a chance for us to start over; the rent is cheap, and it's big enough for all three of us. There's a backyard for Allie to play in, and Mom, please…think about coming with us."

Her mom nodded as Lindsey spoke, her mouth turning down in a frown, then said, "I thought it might be something like that. I had you when I was young, too, and I know it's hard. That's why I wasn't mad when you told me you were pregnant. I knew it wouldn't do you or me any good for me to get angry about it, and I knew how much help you would need. I'll think about it," she said, picking up one of the boxes, then turning and leaving the room.

Lindsey looked around her old bedroom one last time, whispered, "All right then," picked up one of the boxes, and walked from the room.

Outside, with the car packed, Lindsey and her mother hugged one last time. Then Lindsey climbed into the driver's seat, turned to Allie, and asked, "Are you ready, kid?"

Allie shifted in her seat so that she could see her grandma and waved. Then replied in a sullen voice, "Yeah."

"You'll see once we get there, Allie. It's a great house, and you're going to love it," Lindsey said reassuringly.

Lindsey pulled the car away from the mobile home, repeatedly glancing in the rearview mirror, watching as her mother's image grew smaller and smaller. *This is a good move,* she reassured herself. *Mom's going to move to Deep Creek too once she sees how good it is for us there,* she thought as she pressed her foot down on the accelerator, driving them toward the interstate.

The hours and miles passed, and eventually, Allie fell asleep in the passenger seat. Lindsey let her nap until she started to see signs of their exit. Then, excitedly, she woke her, saying, "Allie, we're almost there!"

Allie opened her eyes groggily and said, "It's still the interstate, and it's hot now."

"Yeah, it's summer silly, but this is our exit. See, look," Lindsey said. When they reached their street, Lindsey excitedly pointed out the crepe myrtles that lined the front of each of the three houses there. She slowed the car to a stop in front of the middle house, then leaned over, took a piece of paper from the glove box, and read the address on it, verifying that the middle two-story house was, in fact, the right one. It looked much older to her than the pictures of it online. *Well, it's still a beautiful house,* she thought, *and with the rent so low, I can't complain.* She looked at the houses on each side and noted a light on in the one to the right, but the house on the left appeared vacant. She pulled their car into the driveway, and they got out. Allie excitedly ran to the front porch and peered in the windows. Lindsey followed her more slowly, taking in the small front yard and tidy street. *This is really more than I had hoped for even if it is old,* she thought.

"Mom, how are we going to get in?" Allie called.

"Umm, the realtor said that they left the key in a lockbox on the back door," Lindsey replied. "I have the code. We just have to go around to the back and get the key."

Allie ran to the edge of the porch, jumped down, and headed toward the back of the house.

Lindsey, with her excitement growing, followed her. When she rounded the edge of the house, she stopped and gasped in delight. The backyard was much larger than it had appeared in the pictures, and tall grass about four feet high and three feet deep created a natural fence along the rear of the yard. Past that, there was nothing but a big open field, and she could just make out the edge of what Lindsey assumed was the swamp that she had seen on a map of the area. Lindsey found the lockbox hanging from the back door handle, and she got out the key. Then she and Allie returned to the front door and went inside.

32

Chapter 4

Matilde watched from her kitchen window, her anxiety growing as the young woman and little girl moved into the house next door. When she'd heard the slam of car doors earlier, she had gone to the window to see who had come to visit her but instead had found that a car had pulled into the driveway next door. She'd watched as a little girl bounded up the front porch steps, and a woman who must have been her mother followed close behind, and then she'd watched as they'd entered the house. She had hoped that they would be only prospective tenants and leave, but now, as they carried boxes from their car into the house, those hopes were dashed.

I'll take something over to them, she thought, her unease growing with each passing minute as she set about her kitchen, making a quick casserole dinner to take to the new little family. *I'll go over and introduce myself. If I could get to know them right away, it wouldn't seem odd when, in a few days, I tell them about the town's history and the swamp. I won't make the truth too scary, just enough to warn them away from there.*

An hour and a half later, carrying a piping hot dish of macaroni casserole, Matilde left her house and walked over to her new neighbor's front door. She knocked lightly, then waited and used one of the napkins she had brought with her to wipe the sweat from her brow. She hoped that the woman would assume that the warm evening caused her perspiration and not the truth: that it was her mounting anxiety at their arrival. She knocked again, a little harder this time, and the door opened, revealing a smiling little girl with light brown hair. Matilde smiled back at her and said, "Well, hello there, sweetie. Is your mama home?"

The girl nodded, then slammed the door back closed. Matilde heard her steps running away as she yelled, "Mom, somebody's at the door!"

A few seconds later, the door opened again, and the woman Matilde had seen earlier stood before her. Matilde smiled and said pleasantly, "Hello. My name's Matilde. I live next door, and I couldn't help but notice you and your little girl moving in earlier this evening. I just thought I'd come over and introduce myself and bring over this casserole."

The woman's eyes lit up in surprise as she took the dish from Matilde, saying, " Thank you. My name's Lindsey. It's nice to meet one of the neighbors. Sorry about the door slamming like that."

The girl Matilde had seen earlier appeared at her mother's side, and Matilde gave her a small wave.

Lindsey said, "This is my daughter, Allie. Well, Allison, but we call her Allie for short."

Matilde smiled and said, "I saw you all moving in, and I thought a casserole might be nice to bring over. I know how hard it is to move into a new house and get something on the table for dinner too."

"That's so thoughtful." Lindsey replied, "Have you eaten yet? I don't have much unpacked, but I have some paper plates and plastic forks. We can all share this if you'd like?"

"That's fine by me," Matilde answered, and she followed Lindsey and her little girl, Allie, into the house.

Matilde and Allie sat at the kitchen table while Lindsey dished the casserole onto paper plates and then joined them.

"Did you bring this table with you?" Matilde asked.

"No, I rented the house with some furniture in it. This was really nice of you to bring over," Lindsey said. "I wasn't sure what I was going to make."

Matilde nodded and began eating her food, then said, "My mother and I moved many times when I was a young girl, and I understand how it can be the first day in a new house."

"Oh, does your mother live with you now?" Lindsey asked.

"No, she passed on five years ago," Matilde answered.

"I'm sorry to hear that," Lindsey replied.

"That's all right. It was a long time ago, and she's in a better place now," Matilde said.

"Have you lived in Deep Creek long?" Lindsey asked.

Matilde swallowed a bite of her food and then replied, "Yes, I have been here since I was thirteen years old."

"I bet you know everybody who lives here then," Lindsey said.

"I believe I do," Matilde replied. "It's a quiet town, and most people keep to themselves. But do you know what?" Matilde asked, looking at Allie. "Next month, there will be a parade and fireworks in town on the Fourth of July."

Allie's eyes lit up, and she looked at her mother. "Can we go?" she asked.

"We'll see, but I don't see why not," Lindsey replied.

Matilde took the last bite of casserole from her plate, then said, "Well, I think I'll be going now," and rose from the table.

"Let me make a plate of leftovers for you," Lindsey said, standing as well.

"No, that's for you and your little girl. I just wanted to come over and introduce myself and welcome you to the neighborhood," Matilde answered.

"Well, thank you for coming by and bringing this," Lindsey said.

As Matilde and Lindsey walked to the front door, leaving Allie at the kitchen table to finish her dinner, Matilde said, "If there's anything you need, I live next door. You just come over and knock."

"Thank you, I'll remember that," Lindsey answered.

Matilde left her new neighbors and returned to her house, circling the corner to her backyard. She sat in the swing beside her garden and stared out toward the swamp. Despite the warm evening, she felt chilled. The swing began to slowly rock back and forth, and she whispered, "It's awake."

"It never slept, child," came her mother's voice.

"What do I need to do?" Matilde asked.

"What I always did." came the reply.

"No!" Matilde whispered sharply. "I won't do any work with blood, nothing dark, you know that."

"It's not dark if the deed is for good," she responded.

"I won't feed it off myself," Matilde asserted.

"Not feeding it, child. Binding it," came the reply.

Matilde rose from the swing and walked to her back door. Just as she placed her hand on the knob, she heard her mother's voice next to her ear ask, "If you won't stop it, who will?"

"Somebody else will have to," Matilde asserted, pulling open the door and going inside.

She walked to her mother's room and knelt beside the old cedar chest at the foot of the bed. She ran her hand along the edge of the old wood, then slowly pushed the quilts off the top and opened it. She reached in and took out pillowcases and sheets and set them on the floor beside her, then felt for the latch that would unlock the false bottom that her mother had created there. Finding it, she unhooked the latch and removed the thin plank of cedar, revealing her mother's journals that contained the writings of her encounters with people and their ailments over the years. She pushed these aside, exposing several tins, each with a label taped to it detailing its contents. Matilde knew that on the underside of the lid of each tin, there would be another piece of paper that gave instructions on how to use the mixtures. She poured through the tins, searching for the one her mother had used all those years ago.

"The blue one with the gold pattern," she heard from behind her.

Matilde found it, then sat back and, with trembling fingers, removed the lid. Just as she had known it would be, the tin was filled with the mixture. She shuddered as she remembered the events earlier that morning, and the image of the little girl next door filled her mind. Then, resigning herself to the task, she asked, "When do I have to do it?"

There was no response.

Matilde looked around the room as the answer dawned on her. She would have to do it now.

Matilde went to her kitchen, set the tin down on the counter, and began following the instructions that her mother had left. The sunlight faded, and night came as she worked, grinding together the binding that would keep the thing in its place. When she was done, she placed the contents onto the center of a paper napkin and folded the edges over, creating a small packet. Then she gathered together a matchbook, needle, and her mother's old white candle and left her house through the back door clutching the items tightly to her chest.

She walked determinedly to the edge of her yard and then paused when she reached where she knew her boundary lay. Then, gathering her strength, she boldly stepped past it. She walked quickly at first, then, when she was halfway across, she looked behind her as fear began to creep into her veins, making her want to turn around and run back to her house.

"Keep going," she heard her mother say, urging her forward.

Matilde turned back to the swamp and hurried towards its edge; it seemed to loom before her like a large dark mass against the horizon, blocking out the stars. She dropped to her knees when she reached it, set the white candle and the napkin on the ground in front of her, then took the matchbook from her pocket. She lit the candle and, with shaking fingers, took the needle and quickly pricked her finger. She squeezed until three drops of her blood fell onto the napkin. Then she gently lifted the little bundle, held it over the candle, and watched as it began to burn. As the flame reached the concoction within, smoke began to rise, and a ringing started in her ears. She tilted her head back and closed her eyes as the smoke drifted around her, and the ringing turned into loud voices, chanting that she knew only she could hear. Suddenly, a gust of wind blew past her, extinguishing the flame. Her eyes flew open, and she covered her head with her hands, accidentally dropping the napkin. The air turned icy, and the chanting faded as she cautiously took another match from the box and relit the candle. She frantically searched the ground for the packet; finding it, she held it up to the flame once more. To her dismay, most of the concoction had spilled onto the ground. She quickly burned the rest of the napkin, gathered what she could of what had spilled, and sprinkled it over the flame. Done now, she took the candle in her hand and stood, held the flame high, and peered into the swamp. All seemed still and quiet. Feeling much calmer now that her task was done, she brought the candle to her lips and blew out the flame. Darkness immediately surrounded her, and almost dreamily, she took a step forward. She was vaguely aware of her mother's voice screaming in her head, but she couldn't make out the words as she slowly walked into the swamp.

The darkness and a warm breeze enveloped her like the softest of blankets and gently propelled her forward. Soon, she came to a clearing where she saw the night sky beautifully reflected on the surface of a pond. Time lost all meaning for her as she stood admiring the reflection. Then, suddenly, a shock of icy cold enveloped her foot and ran up her leg. She looked down and saw with horror that she had taken a step into the pond. The spell over her was broken, and she jerked her foot out of the water and staggered backward, then turned and ran blindly into the trees. She could feel the presence of her mother with her now and heard her voice saying fervently, "This way, this way," guiding Matilde back out of the swamp.

When she reached the field, she ran to her house as quickly as she could, went into the bathroom, turned on the hot water in the shower, and got in. Then, she sat on the bottom of the tub, massaging her still-cold foot.

Tears clouded her vision, and she sobbed quietly, saying, "I didn't get it all burned."

After showering, she returned to her mother's room and repacked everything into the cedar chest. Then, taking the quilts with her, she went to her bed and lay down. Hours passed, and she couldn't find sleep. She went over and over the details of what had happened in her mind and hoped that the amount of binding that she had burned would be enough to keep the thing in its place.

Chapter 5

Allie picked her jump rope up off the ground and started twirling it. It was just after breakfast, and she played alone in Matilde's backyard. She and her mother had moved to their new house four weeks ago, and although her mom had taken her to the park and around the town, Allie had yet to make any friends. Her mom had found a job, and now Matilde watched her during the day. Allie wanted to be babysat at her house next door, where more of her toys were, but Matilde insisted that she watch Allie in her own home.

Allie, tiring of her jump rope, dropped it and skipped over to Matilde's large garden. She wandered up and down the rows, kneeling occasionally to examine the clusters of cherry tomatoes and large blossoms on the squash plants. A movement just past the yard's edge caught her eye, and she turned to see what it was. At first, she saw nothing but the waving of the tall maiden grass that lined the back of Matilde's yard; she walked from between the garden rows and moved closer to the grass, sure that she had seen something. A breeze blew, parting the grass, and Allie exclaimed, "Oh!" when she saw the figure of a girl about her age kneeling there. Allie tentatively waved her hand and called. "Hello…"

The girl looked at Allie questioningly but didn't answer.

Uncertain what to do next, Allie said, "I'm Allie."

The girl still said nothing and only gazed at Allie as if she were unsure whether she should respond.

"Well, do you wanna play with me?" Allie asked tentatively, taking a few slow steps towards the girl, who stood up as Allie approached. Allie saw that she was indeed close to her age and about the same height. She said, "I have a jump rope, and you can jump with me if you want." Then she asked, "Hey, what's your name?"

The girl smiled and moved to take a step toward Allie but then stopped and knelt back down.

"Allison?" Allie heard Matilde call from the kitchen window.

"Yeah?" she called back, turning towards the house.

"What are you doing over there?" Matilde asked.

Allie looked back toward the girl, who knelt on the ground, holding one finger to her lips as though to say be quiet.

Allie smiled, then responded, "Nothing."

"Well, bring that nothing you're doing closer to the house. You stay in the yard now," Matilde instructed.

"I will," Allie answered. She watched as Matilde moved away from the window and then turned back to her new friend, but she was gone. "Hey!" Allie whispered loudly. "Don't go, let's play." She rushed into the maiden grass and was about to step past it when she heard Matilde call again from the house.

"Allie, that's too far. You need to come back in the yard!"

"I won't go far, Matilde, I promise. I wanna see…" she paused.

"What do you want to see?" Matilde asked, stepping out of the house and onto the back porch.

Allie looked around for the girl but didn't see her. She responded to Matilde, "Nothin'," and then went to stand beside her.

"What were you doing all the way back over there?" Matilde asked. "Now you know I asked you not to go back that far. These old eyes can't see you that far from the house, and it's my job to watch over you while your mom's at work."

"I know," Allie said. "I just don't have anything to do here," she responded.

Matilde considered what Allie had said for a minute. She could feel that the girl was hiding something, but deciding not to press the issue, she said, "How about this? Once I'm done cleaning up these breakfast dishes, we'll go over to your house pick up one of your board games and play it together. How does that sound?"

Allie smiled, the girl forgotten momentarily, and replied, "Yes."

"All right then, you go on in the house and turn on some cartoons, and just as soon as I'm done, we'll go get that game," Matilde said.

The rest of the day passed lazily. Later that evening, as Allie swung on the swing set her mother had set up for her in their backyard, she stared at the empty house next door. *I wonder what it's like in there,* she thought. Then, giving in to her curiosity, she jumped from her swing and walked to the empty house. She cupped her hands around her eyes and peered in the windows, then ran back and forth across the front porch. Then, when she grew tired of that, she went to the front door and rang the doorbell. She knocked on the door and called out playfully, "Anybody home?" then grabbed the doorknob and turned it. To her surprise, it opened. Allie gave a small gasp and jumped back, then moved closer to go inside. The house was laid out much like her own. She wandered through the empty rooms, then climbed the stairs to the second floor, where she found that one of the bedrooms was still furnished with an old bed and bedside table that were covered in a thick layer of dust. It looked to her as though the room used to belong to a child. The walls were a pale green, and on the bed was a blanket with a pattern of trains on it. She thought *I wonder why they left their kid's stuff but took all their other things*. Allie walked to the closet, where, to her surprise, she found toys and a boy's clothes hanging on hangers. "That's weird," she said softly.

Suddenly, Allie heard the bedroom door creak behind her, and she jumped and whirled around. To her shock, the little girl she had seen earlier that day stood in the doorway.

"Oh, how did you get in here?" Allie asked, surprised. Then, remembering that she shouldn't be in the empty house herself, she asked hesitantly, "Is this your house?"

The little girl beamed a smile at Allie and emphatically shook her head no.

Allie laughed nervously and then asked, "What's your name?"

The girl held up one hand, her palm facing Allie then lowered it to her side.

Confused, Allie said, "I don't get it."

The girl tilted her head then held her hand up again.

"Ohh," Allie said. "You can't talk, can you."

The girl smiled at Allie again and shook her head no.

"Well, that's okay," Allie said. "There was a boy in my last school who couldn't talk either but could play. Do you wanna play?" she asked.

The girl nodded enthusiastically, and Allie moved to the closet and started pulling out some of the dust-covered toys.

"We can play with some of these. They're old, but I think we can still come up with a game to play," she said

The girl came to stand beside her at the closet and watched as Allie moved some of the toys to the center of the room. Then, together, they sat down and used the old blocks and little metal race cars to build a small town.

After a while, Allie heard her mom's voice calling her from outside. "Oh, that's my mom. I gotta go," she said.

The two girls stood, and Allie dusted her hands off on her skirt, then asked, "Do you want to play again tomorrow?"

The little girl nodded her head yes.

"I sure wish you could tell me your name," Allie said.

The little girl stepped back and made the same motion with her hand, holding it up as though to signal stop.

"I'm sorry," Allie said, "but I don't know what that means. I don't know anything about sign language, but I can ask my mom. Maybe she knows. Do you wanna meet here at the same time tomorrow, and we can play again?" Allie asked

The girl made a face as though she was thinking, and then moved to the window and pointed outside.

Allie went to stand beside her and looked out the window to see what she was pointing at but didn't notice anything but the field and the giant swamp past it. "I don't get it. You wanna play in the field?" she asked. She heard her mom call her name again and said, "I'll be back here tomorrow, and we can play here, okay?" Then she added, "Hey, do you live around here?"

The little girl smiled, nodded yes, and pointed again out the window.

"Okay, well then, I'll see you tomorrow," Allie said and leaned forward to hug her new friend. "Oh! You're freezing," she exclaimed.

Her new friend just shrugged her shoulders.

Allie quickly left the house and ran towards her mom's voice. She found her standing in their backyard, and as Allie came closer, she demanded, "Where were you?"

"I was over there playing," Allie huffed, gesturing toward the empty house next door.

"Stay closer so I can see you next time," Lindsey said. "I was worried. I've been calling you for five minutes."

"Okay," Allie agreed quickly.

Lindsey smiled at her daughter and asked, "Guess what?"

"What?" Allie asked.

"Grandma's coming this weekend for the Fourth of July, and she's going to stay until Sunday night," she said.

Allie shrieked and jumped, then said, "Hey, she can meet my new friend."

"What new friend?" Lindsey asked, looking around, "Did you meet somebody out here?"

"Yeah, I met another girl. She lives…somewhere around here," Allie replied.

"Did you meet her just now? Is she nearby?" Lindsey asked, looking around questioningly.

"Yeah, I met her just now, and we were playing, but she lives somewhere around here." Then she asked, "Mom, do you know sign language?"

"What? No, I don't know sign language. Why do you ask that?" Lindsey asked.

"Because she can't talk, she uses her hands instead," Allie replied.

"Oh," Lindsey said. "Well, I don't know any, but maybe you should go ask your new friend if she needs a ride home."

Allie hesitated before answering. She would have to go back in the house to ask her friend if she needed a ride, and her mom would surely see her go inside, she might even walk with her, and she didn't want her mom to know that she had been playing not outside of the empty house but upstairs in one of the bedrooms, so she said, "She already left. She walked towards town."

"All right, then," Lindsey said. "Let's go back in the house and get you ready for bed."

Upstairs in her room, as Allie lay waiting for sleep, she thought over her day. She was happy that she had met someone to play with. She hadn't said anything to her mom, but she had been worried that she would have to start her new school without knowing a single person.

49

Chapter 6

Allie's grandma pulled her old Chevy Nova into the house's driveway early Friday morning on the Fourth of July weekend. She got out and leaned against the front of her car, admiring her daughter's rented house and the quiet street. She took her sunglasses off and placed them on the top of her head, thinking, *this really is nicer than where I'm at. I could see us all living here for a while.*

Suddenly, the front door of the house burst open, and Allie ran out with her arms spread wide, yelling, "Grandma! Grandma!"

"Allie!" she yelled back, opening her arms and catching the girl as she flew into them.

Lindsey walked out onto the porch and said, "Hi, Mom, I've got breakfast cooking in here. Come in and eat."

Allie released her grandma and took her by the hand, pulling her towards the house, saying, "Come on, Mom made something special for you."

In the kitchen, they all sat down to Lindsey's breakfast of pancakes, bacon, scrambled eggs, and hashbrowns.

"You didn't have to go through all this trouble for me, Lindsey," she said.

"I know, but I wanted to," Lindsey replied.

"Well, this meal is really something and it looks like you've done really well for yourself here, girl."

Lindsey smiled, hoping that the house, the town, and the breakfast would make a big impression on her mom so that she would change her mind and move to Deep Creek. "I just wanted to do something nice," she said.

"So, what's this I hear on the phone about a parade and fireworks this weekend?" she asked, looking at Allie.

"There's going to be a parade tomorrow morning, and later on, when it gets dark, there are going to be fireworks, and we're going to go to the park with a blanket and sit and watch them with everybody else in the town," Allie replied excitedly.

"Now that sounds like something I'd like to do," she replied.

Lindsey glanced at her watch and said, "Mom, I want to stay with you longer, but you know I have to work today…"

"No, that's fine. I know it's only Friday. It's not the end of the week yet. You go on, and I'll settle myself in, and Allie and I will have a great day here at the house."

"Thanks, Mom," Lindsey said. "I hate to run, but I have to get to work."

"Don't you worry about it," she said, reaching and squeezing Lindsey's hand.

"The neighbor, Matilde, might come by and introduce herself. I told her that you were coming today," Lindsey said.

"Who is this woman you've told me so much about? She sounds like a nice lady."

"She really is. I don't think I've ever met anybody so easy to talk to and helpful," Lindsey replied.

"I'm glad for it. From what you've told me, she's been a real blessing to you here."

Lindsey nodded yes, picked up her plate and took it to the kitchen sink, then grabbed her purse and car keys, kissed her mom on the cheek, and left.

"Well, it's just you and me now, Allie," she said. "What should we do today?"

Allie jumped up from the table and grabbed her grandma's hand, pulling on it and saying, "Come and see my room."

"Just let me put my fork down, and I'm coming," she replied laughingly as she rose from the table.

She followed Allie upstairs, where Allie showed her the new things her mom had gotten her since she'd started her job in town. Then she showed her the sparklers Lindsey had bought them to light at the park.

"I have something for you, too, Allie," she said.

"You do?" Allie asked excitedly

"Yes, but I left it in my car. I'll run out and get it and be right back."

She left the house and went to her car, retrieved the little lilac-colored purse with a shoulder strap that she had gotten for Allie, then returned to the house. She was about to re-enter Allie's room when she saw her through the open door, gazing dreamily out the bedroom window. Something about the way she stood concerned her; it was almost as though she were asleep on her feet. She entered the room and walked slowly to stand behind Allie, who hummed quietly and didn't seem to notice her. She gently touched Allie's shoulder and asked, "Honey?"

Allie jumped and looked up at her, replying in a groggy voice, "Grandma."

"Honey, are you okay?" she asked, kneeling down and touching Allie's forehead to see if she was feverish and coming down with something.

"I'm fine," she said, brushing away her grandma's hand.

"Well, what were you doing?" she asked.

"Nothing, just listening to the music," Allie replied.

Her brow wrinkled in confusion, and she stepped closer to the window, opening it and listening. She hadn't heard any music when she'd been outside and knew the television in the living room wasn't turned on. "I don't hear anything, Allie," she said.

"I think it was just my friend. She sings sometimes," Allie answered.

"Ohh," her grandma replied. "Is she outside? You can have her come in, and then we can all spend the day together if you want."

"No, she's shy," Allie sighed.

"Maybe next time, then," she said, handing Allie the gift she had brought. "Here you go. I hope you like it."

Allie shrieked in happiness. "I love it," she said as she took the gift from her grandma's hand placed the shoulder strap over her shoulder and walked around the room.

After a while, her grandma asked, "Do you want me to drive us into town, and you can show me around?"

"Yes," Allie said.

They drove into town, walked down the main street, and Allie pointed out all the shops she and her mom had visited. They got ice cream at the parlor and then went to the park, where they would watch fireworks the next day and Allie played on the playground equipment while her grandma rested on a bench.

Later that evening, when they were back at the house, she asked her daughter, "Have you met Allie's new friend yet?"

"No," Lindsey replied, "and I haven't seen her yet either. I was starting to think that Allie just made her up because she hadn't met anybody here yet, and there aren't a lot of kids in the town, but Allie insists that she's just a timid little girl."

"She said that she heard her singing today when she was in her bedroom. I had left her up there when I went to my car to get the gift that I had brought her, and when I came back, she was standing by her window with the oddest look on her face, almost like she was asleep. I went to her and put my hand on her shoulder, and she said that she'd been listening to music, but I thought she must be coming down with something because there was no music and she seemed like she wasn't herself."

"Did you check her temperature?" Lindsey asked.

"Yeah, I touched her forehead, and she didn't feel hot, but it was just the oddest thing. She said she was listening to her friend singing."

"That is odd. I'll have to watch her and make sure she's not coming down with something," she replied, brushing off her mother's concerns.

Upstairs in her room, Allie sat on her bed petting a toy kitten. The room was stuffy, and she moved to her window to open it. To her surprise, she saw their neighbor, Matilde, strolling along the back of their yard carrying something in one hand. Allie squinted her eyes, peering closer to see what it was. She realized it was a bowl, and that Matilde was scooping something out of it and sprinkling it on the ground. Allie considered calling to her to ask her what she was doing but thought better of it, deciding that she probably wouldn't tell her what she was up to anyway.

Allie looked past Matilde to the swamp where she now knew that her friend lived alone. She wondered if it was scary for her by herself in there. She wondered if maybe that was why, lately, when she and her friend were playing together, she frequently gestured for Allie to follow her into the swamp. Allie had told Matilde about her friend, and Matilde had become very upset and warned Allie away from the little girl, saying that this friend wasn't a nice girl at all, but she had never been mean to Allie, so she had continued to play with her.

Allie wondered now if her friend could see the light from her bedroom window from where she lived in the swamp, and she lifted her hand and waved.

56

Chapter 7

Moonlight filtered through it and glistened off the top of the pond as it lay spread out across the water, waiting for the sun to rise and the little one to wake.

An owl hooted in the distance, and it turned its attention to it, then gathered itself together and moved toward the sound until it found the small creature on the branch of a tree. It watched as the owl swooped down from its perch to grasp a mouse in its sharp talons. The owl held the mouse in its vice-like grip and then used its sharp beak to deliver a quick fatal blow to the mouse's neck, killing the creature; then it carried the mouse back to its perch and began eating.

It left the owl to its meal and returned to the pond. The images of the kill kept coming back to it, the mouse's crushed body completely still, with its life gone. It compared this mouse to the small skeletal forms it held at the bottom of its pond, wondering for the first time if it wouldn't be better to exist with the small ones rather than keep them forever with it.

It had never attempted to exist alongside anything that lived outside the swamp before, nor had it ever traveled beyond a perimeter of roughly two miles from the swamp's edge, finding it too difficult to maintain its form the farther away from its pond that it got. It looked back through its long memory to the different times it had existed with other creatures. There had been the snapping turtle that, for a time, had carried it slowly throughout the swamp within the chamber of its lung. It had been a voracious eater and foraged for food day and night, which, not being something that consumed food itself, Silence had enjoyed.

It had flown with numerous types of wildlife through the skies, again carried within the cavities of their chests. This space where air moved in and out was the one thing all living creatures seemed to have in common, where it could make itself very small and reside. It had always had to leave them when they flew far away from the swamp, forced to expand from its smaller form and exit through their mouths when the concentration it took to stay small became too great as the distance from its home grew farther. It considered that humans, as animals, would also have this open chamber within their chests.

It shifted and moved along the top of the water as it thought about what it would be like to live alongside one of the small ones.

Chapter 8

The morning of the Fourth of July dawned brightly with a cloudless sky and stifling humidity. Lindsey sat on the couch in her living room, waiting for her mom to return from the grocery store with the items they would pack for their picnic lunch after the parade. Allie still slept peacefully in her room. Lindsey slowly sipped her coffee, enjoying a few moments of rest before the day's festivities began.

The front door opened, and Lindsey's mom walked in carrying bags of groceries.

"What all did you get?" Lindsey asked, setting her coffee cup down and rising from the couch to take some of the bags from her.

"Just a few things, some stuff I thought everybody would like," her mom replied as she handed Lindsey some of the bags.

They took the groceries into the kitchen and put them on the table, where a picnic basket sat ready to be packed.

Lindsey emptied one of the bags, removed lunchmeat, drinks, and chips, and then withdrew a pair of star-shaped sunglasses. She put them on, turned to her mom, and made a funny face.

"Those are for Allie," her mom said, smiling.

Lindsey took off the sunglasses and said, "We better go ahead and make the sandwiches now." Then she asked, "Do you think we should go back home after the parade or stay and wait for the fireworks?"

"Well, it's going to be pretty hot, Lindsey. We should probably come back to the house, and then we can go out for the fireworks later," her mom said, adding, "Is your neighbor coming with us?"

Lindsey shook her head no as she started putting the sandwiches together, "I invited her, but she said it's too hot. She might come out later for the fireworks, though."

Allie walked into the kitchen then, her hair tangled from sleep, and sat at the table.

Her grandma picked up the star-shaped sunglasses and put them on Allie.

Allie giggled, then said, "I'm hungry."

"Get yourself a bowl from the cupboard, and I'll pour you some cereal," Lindsey replied. "Right after breakfast, we're heading into town, so when you're done eating, you go ahead and get dressed. I want to get there a little early so we get a good seat."

An hour later, they piled into Lindsey's car and drove into town, where they watched the festively decorated floats drive slowly by, and Allie collected several of the handfuls of candy that were thrown out for the children to catch. After the parade, they went to the park and enjoyed their picnic. Then, as the sun climbed high in the sky and the heat began to soar, Lindsey turned to her mom and said, "I think we should probably go back to the house. I'm starting to burn up."

Her mom nodded in agreement and called to Allie playing on the playground. They packed up their picnic and drove back home.

When they got there Allie rushed from the car towards the back of the house.

"Hey girl, where are you going?" Lindsey yelled from the driver's side window.

"To play!" Allie called back over her shoulder.

"She never sits still," Lindsey remarked.

"You never did either," her mom replied as she stepped from the car.

Inside the house, Lindsey said, "I think I'll watch some TV before the fireworks."

"I'll join you. Do you want me to call Allie inside so we can watch something together?" her mom asked.

"No, just let her go play and get some of her energy out," Lindsey replied.

Outside, Allie ran immediately through the maiden grass at the back of the yard and into the field. She could just make out the shape of her friend standing by this swamp and hurried toward her. When she reached her, she moved to take her hand, saying, "Come over to my house and meet my grandma."

Her friend pulled her hand away and stepped backward towards the swamp.

"What's wrong?" Allie asked. "Don't you want to play with me?"

Her friends smiled and nodded yes, then took another step toward the swamp.

"Well, come on then, let's go!" Allie said excitedly, reaching for her friend's hand again. But instead of letting her take it, her friend spun around and ran into the swamp. "Hey, where are you going? I can't go in there," Allie yelled as her friend moved farther away. Allie glanced hesitantly back over her shoulder towards her house. Then, making up her mind, she said, "OK, we can go to your house this time, but I want you to come over and meet my grandma later. Hey, wait for me!"

An hour later, Matilde heard someone calling her name and knocking frantically at her back door. She rose from her chair, saying, "I'm coming! Who is it?" Then she winced as a sharp pain shot through the left side of her head, and an image of Allie filled her mind. She hurried to her door and opened it to find Lindsey standing there, her eyes wide.

"My mom and I can't find Allie. Is she here?" she asked in a shaky voice.

Matilde gasped and covered her mouth as the image of Allie faded. She replied, "No, she isn't here. Have you checked that empty house on the other side of yours?"

"I already looked there," Lindsey replied hurriedly.

Her fear began to mount as Matilde asked, "Did you check the swamp?"

"Allie wouldn't go in the swamp," Lindsey replied.

Matilde said urgently, "Go straight back from your house. Cross the field. You'll see a little path. It looks like it's an animal trail, but it takes you to a pond. Follow that path. Check there."

Lindsey started to shake her head no, but Matilde insisted, saying, "Check! It's a hot day. She might have gone in thinking she could cool off there. You haven't found her any place else, have you?"

Lindsey interjected, "But Allie can't swim! She wouldn't be there."

"Then you better run," Matilde replied solemnly.

Lindsey turned away from Matilde and looked out toward the swamp, reasoning with herself that although Allie couldn't swim, she had, as Matilde said, already looked everywhere else, and she started running toward the swamp.

"Where are you going?" Lindsey heard her mom yell behind her.

She didn't answer but sped up as a ball of dread began to form in the pit of her stomach. She quickly located the thin trail and followed it to a clearing where, just like Matilde had said there would be, there was a pond. Her eyes darted around frantically in search of Allie. She heard someone crashing through the swamp behind her, and her mom came to stand at her side. They both started searching the area, and then Lindsey heard her mom scream. She turned to see her pointing toward the pond. Lindsey looked where she pointed and, to her horror, saw her daughter floating face down in the water. She ran toward her, crashing into the water with her mom close behind her. They reached Allie, quickly flipped her over, and pulled her back to shore, where Lindsey lay Allie on her back and began breathing into her mouth.

"Oh my God!" Lindsey's mom sobbed uncontrollably.

Lindsey continued to repeatedly breathe into her daughter's mouth until, suddenly, Allie coughed, and water poured from her mouth and nose. Lindsey quickly turned her to her side and started patting her back, saying, "Come on, Allie! Just breathe. Come on!"

Allie choked forth more water, and then opened her eyes.

Lindsey pushed the wet hair back from Allie's face and, cradling her head, said, "Can you hear me? Say something, Allie!"

Allie didn't answer.

Lindsey pulled her daughter into a sitting position, then grasped her firmly under each arm, saying, "Mom, grab her feet. We have to get her to a hospital."

Together, they carried Allie out of the swamp as quickly as they could. They were halfway back across the field when Lindsey's mom could carry Allie no farther, and she fell to her knees. Lindsey saw Matilde running towards them, and she lowered Allie the rest of the way to the ground.

"Stay with her," Lindsey said as Matilde reached them. "I'm going to call 911," she said and sprinted towards her house.

Matilde knelt on the ground beside Allie, took her hand in her own, and then, shocked at the coldness of her flesh, immediately dropped it. She leaned close to Allie's face, examining the girl's features, noticing the pallor of her skin and unfocused eyes. She bent forward to hear Allie's breathing and make sure that the girl was indeed alive, as the slight movements of her body suggested but the coldness of her flesh denied. As she paused there listening, Allie's eyes focused, and she looked at Matilde. Matilde jerked backward.

"What is it?" Lindsey's mom asked.

"I think she's awake now," Matilde answered.

Lindsey's mom pulled Allie to her, placed her head on her lap, and said, "Help's coming soon, baby. Can you say something to me, Allie? Can you hear me?"

Allie coughed and wretched again, making various noises as she attempted to speak.

"Take your time," Matilde said soothingly. "Just take your time. Try one word. Try your name. Can you say your name for me?"

Allie jerked her head towards Matilde and croaked out, "Silence."

Chapter 9

One month later, Lindsey sat at the kitchen table with Allie having breakfast. Her mom, who had moved in with them permanently after Allie's accident, was in the backyard with a hoe and tiller, working to start a garden like their neighbor Matilde's. Lindsey heard Matilde now talking with her mom, and she glanced up as her backdoor opened, and Matilde walked in. Allie looked up at her, then rose from the table and left the room. Matilde watched her go, then pulled out a chair and sat down.

"Hi, Matilde," Lindsey said tiredly.

"Good morning," Matilde replied. She glanced in the direction Allie had gone, then asked, "How is she doing? Any better?"

Lindsey shook her head and said, "She has her good days and bad days. Lucky for me, today was one of her good days, and she got some of this breakfast down."

"It'll probably just take some time, is all," Matilde said, then added, "Is she talking yet?"

Lindsey sighed and shook her head. "Just a few words here and there, but not much. You know what, Matilde? Sometimes I think she's trying to say something to me but can't get it out. Like when I'm tucking her into bed at night. She looks at me with such an intense look in her eyes, almost like she's scared or something, and I stay in her room with her until she falls asleep, but she doesn't make a sound, and something else that's real odd is she doesn't want to leave the house. This little girl puts up such a fight to not go out, and look at my arm," Lindsey said, rolling up the sleeve of her shirt exposing four long red scratches on her forearm. "This is what she did when I had to take her to her appointment three days ago."

Matilde looked at the angry marks and slowly shook her head. "You need to put some ointment on those," she said. "I have something I made myself that you can use, and hopefully, it won't leave a scar." She paused momentarily and asked, "How have you and your mom been?"

"Mom's been great," Lindsey replied. "She helps with everything."

"That's good. It's always nice when someone has a mother to lean on. If you want, I can keep an eye on Allie anytime so that the two of you can have a break," Matilde offered.

"Thank you, Matilde. I'll keep that in mind," Lindsey replied, rising from the table. "I don't want to rush you off, but I need to get down to the hardware store and pick up fencing to go around the garden. Mom's been asking for some."

Matilde rose and said, "Well, I'll let myself out the front door. I know the way."

She left the kitchen and walked into the living room, where Allie sat on the couch watching cartoons. As she walked past her, she noticed that Allie glanced at her out of the corner of her eye. Matilde turned, faced the little girl, and said, "I see you watching me, Allie, and I know you're in there. Don't worry; we'll find a way to get it out." Then she added in a lower, mean tone, "And I see you too...Silence."

Allie slowly turned her head toward Matilde and narrowed her eyes to glare at the older woman.

Matilde held the girl's unnatural gaze for a few seconds, then turned and left the house.

71

Epilogue

Later that evening, Matilde strolled quietly in the town's old graveyard, humming gently to herself and stopping occasionally to place a wildflower from the basket that she carried on the tops of the smallest headstones. She wove her way to the center of the graveyard, where a tall weeping willow stood, and sat down under the swaying branches. She set her basket beside her, watched as fog gathered, and smiled, knowing it brought her visitors. She took a glass jar from her basket and a small hand shovel, then began digging clumps of dirt from the ground and placing it in the jar. She heard the giggle of a child and glanced up to see the face of a small boy smiling at her from between the swaying branches of the willow tree.

"Hello there," she whispered and smiled back.

The boy tilted his head and gave a small wave as his image became brighter, then faded away.

Matilde returned to her task. When the jar was full, she placed it back in her basket, gathered her things, and walked out from beneath the tree. The fog was thicker now, and she could hear children's voices playing within it. The cheerful sounds rang to her from the other side like a balm soothing her nerves, which had become frayed since Allie's accident. As she wove her way back through the graveyard, her thoughts turned to Allie and what she knew in her heart to be true: that the thing from the swamp now resided within her. It made her shudder to think that such a thing could be possible. She had gone through her mother's old cedar chest many times, looking for something that would cast the thing out, but had found nothing useful. Her mother had also been eerily quiet, and although Matilde often felt her presence, her words were few. She reached out to her now, "If there's something you know I can do to help her, why don't you tell me?" she whispered. Matilde stopped walking and closed her eyes, concentrating intently as she waited for a reply, but none came. Matilde sighed deeply, then said loudly, "Well, I can't just leave it within her!" The harshness with which she spoke her words caused the tinkling of the children's voices to stop and the fog to begin to dissipate. "There has to be something!" she shouted angrily into the empty air, shaking her basket. Again, there was no reply.

She scoffed, aggravated by the continued quiet, and started walking again. She was almost outside the graveyard when she heard her mother call, "Matilde."

Matilde turned towards the voice and waited for more words to come.

"You won't do it," she heard. "It would be dark."

"I'll get somebody else to do it," she hissed. "Just tell me who to go to, but don't leave this little girl like this!"

"Nobody else is so close," came her mother's reply.

"Just tell me who to go to," she insisted.

"Then you don't love her. Let it lie," came the reply.

Matilde's thoughts raced over the events that had transpired since Lindsey and Allie had moved in next door. She remembered the times she and Allie had spent together and her growing fondness for her. Matilde was surprised to realize that she had, in fact, come to love the little girl whose eyes sometimes cried out to her for help.

"Or do you?" her mother asked.

Matilde shuddered as she considered what the few words her mother said implied, then asked, "How dark would it be?"

The wind picked up, but no reply came.

Later that night, as she lay in bed, Matilde tossed and turned, unable to find sleep. She knew that she would help Allie, but she didn't know what the cost to herself would be. All she knew was that helping Allie would mean asking for something from the darker realm, and just like the drops of blood on the packet of Binding, she would have to give something of herself in return.